W9-ASK-657

Contents

4

Private Eye at Work

Gumshoe Goose, the ace detective,

was sitting in his office.

He was polishing his spyglass.

"Business is slow today," he said.

"I'll telephone my father,

Inspector Goose, at the jail.

Maybe he can use some help."

"Hello, Father," said Gumshoe.

"This is your son, G. Goose,

the ace detective."

"Who?" asked Inspector Goose.

"Your son, Gumshoe,"

said Gumshoe Goose.

"Stop playing detective,

Gumshoe," said his father.

"Get yourself a real job."

"This *is* my real job,"

said Gumshoe Goose.

"But I am not busy today.

Can I help you solve a crime?"

"No," said Inspector Goose.

"But watch out for Fat Fox,

Public Enemy Number One.

There is always trouble

when he comes to town."

Gumshoe looked out the window.

Fat Fox was nowhere in sight.

"Looking for Public Enemy Number One makes my eyes tired," he said.

Gumshoe yawned.

Then he leaned back

in his chair.

He put his feet up on the desk

and closed his eyes.

Zzzzzzz, snored Gumshoe Goose.

Public Enemy
Number One

Fat Fox was hungry.

"Granny," he said,

"where is my breakfast?"

"I can't see," said Granny Fox.

"I have lost my glasses.

I can't cook until I find them."

"They are on your forehead,"
said Fat Fox.

"Oh, deary me!" cried Granny.
She pulled down her glasses
and set about making breakfast.

Fat Fox ate everything

on his plate.

"That tasted *great*!"

he said.

"What was it, Granny?"

"Fried worms on toast,"
said Granny Fox.

"Yuck!" muttered Fat Fox.

"What's for lunch?" he asked.

"Snake stew with lizard dumplings,"
said Granny.

"Double yuck!" growled Fat Fox.

"What we need around here
is some decent grub," he said.
"I'm going to town to get
something good for our dinner."
"While you are gone I think
I will take a nap," said Granny.
Fat Fox smiled his foxy smile.

When Granny fell asleep, Fat Fox took
off her glasses and put them on.
Then he put on her shawl and
took her shopping basket.

Fat Fox sang a cheery tune as he started off to town.

"Chicken for breakfast,

Chicken for lunch.

Chicken anytime

Is great to munch," he sang.

Suddenly he saw Mrs. Hen coming

down the road.

Fat Fox jumped behind a bush.

Mrs. Hen went into the bakery.

Fat Fox listened at the door.

"I would like to buy a chocolate

birthday cake," said Mrs. Hen.

"It is for Baby Chick-Chick.

He is one month old today."

Fat Fox's mouth began to water.

"Chicken and dumplings,

Chicken and rice.

Little Baby Chick-Chick

Will taste very nice!" he whispered.

Inspector Goose came out of the jail.

"Good morning, Granny Fox," he said.

"Where is Fat Fox today?"

"Sleeping late," said Fat Fox

in his old granny voice.

Then he hurried down the road.

Fat Fox peeked in

Gumshoe Goose's window.

Gumshoe was taking a nap.

"This is my lucky day!" cried Fat Fox.

"Fried chicken,

Chicken in the pot.

Stewed Baby Chick-Chick,

Get it while it's hot!" he sang.

Then he ran down the road and
knocked on the henhouse door.

"Go away!" yelled Baby Chick-Chick.
"I'm not allowed to open
the door to strangers."

"It's Granny Fox," said Fat Fox

in his old granny voice.

"I have a birthday surprise for you."

Baby Chick-Chick opened the door

and Fat Fox stepped inside.

"Where is my birthday surprise?"
asked Baby Chick-Chick.
"SURPRISE!" yelled Fat Fox.

He popped Baby Chick-Chick into
the basket and closed the lid.

Fat Fox started to make his getaway.

Suddenly he thought of the cake.

"What a waste," said Fat Fox.

He loved chocolate cake almost

as much as chicken.

Fat Fox smiled his foxy smile.

"Maybe I can have the cake and

Baby Chick-Chick too," he said.

Fat Fox sat down at the table
and took off Granny's glasses.
He wrote a note to Mrs. Hen.
Just then Fat Fox heard Mrs. Hen
coming up the walk.

He grabbed the shopping basket
and jumped out the window.
He ran across a field and into
the woods to Granny's house.

Calling Gumshoe Goose

"Wake up, Gumshoe Goose!"
yelled Mrs. Hen.

"Who's sleeping?" said Gumshoe.

"I was just resting my eyes."

"Baby Chick-Chick has been
kidnapped," cried Mrs. Hen.

"What shall I do, Gumshoe Goose?"

Gumshoe Goose stood up and bowed.

He was not only an ace detective

—he was a goose with good manners.

"What happened?" he asked.

"Well," said Mrs. Hen, crying,

"I left Baby Chick-Chick at home

while I went shopping.

"Then I went to the bakery

to buy a chocolate cake."

"Please," sighed Gumshoe,

"just give me the facts."

"These are the facts," she said.

"When I came home with the cake,

Baby Chick-Chick was gone.

I found this note on my table."

"Hmmmm," said Gumshoe Goose.

"Very interesting.

G. Goose will take the case."

Gumshoe telephoned the jail.

"Father," he said, "I am working

on a kidnapping case."

"Gumshoe," said Inspector Goose,

"that is police work."

"Right, Father," said Gumshoe.

"Meet me at the henhouse."

The Case of the Hungry Kidnapper

"Is this the scene of the crime?"
asked Inspector Goose at the henhouse.

"Yes," said Gumshoe Goose.

"I am calling this the Case of
the Hungry Kidnapper!"

"What does food have to do with
this case?" asked the Inspector.

Gumshoe handed him the note.

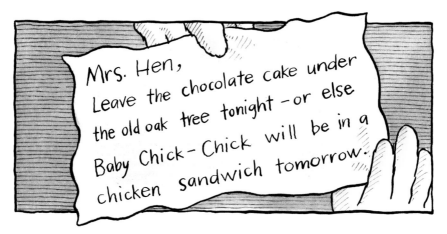

Mrs. Hen,
Leave the chocolate cake under
the old oak tree tonight – or else
Baby Chick-Chick will be in a
chicken sandwich tomorrow.

"Don't worry, Mrs. Hen,"

said Inspector Goose.

"I will catch the kidnapper."

He ran back to the jail to get

his handcuffs.

Gumshoe Goose wrote in his black book:

Clue Number One: open window.

Clue Number Two: chocolate cake.

Inspector Goose came back with
the handcuffs.

"Where is Gumshoe?" he asked.

"Under the table," said Mrs. Hen.

"Son," yelled Inspector Goose,

"why are you under the table?"

"I'm looking for Clue Number Three,"

said Gumshoe.

"Stop looking for clues,"

said Inspector Goose.

"I have cracked this case.

Granny Fox is the kidnapper.

I saw her come into town.

Follow me!" he cried.

Gumshoe and Mrs. Hen followed the
Inspector to Granny Fox's house.

They burst through the door.

Granny was asleep in her rocker.

Baby Chick-Chick was on the stove.

Fat Fox was adding salt and pepper.

"Ah-choo!" sneezed Baby Chick-Chick.

"My baby!" cried Mrs. Hen.

"Wake up, Granny, you are under arrest!"
yelled Inspector Goose.

"Wait, Father," said Gumshoe,

"you have the wrong fox."

"Don't argue," said his father.

"I watched the road all day.

Only Granny came into town."

"Wrong, Father," said Gumshoe.

"It only looked like Granny.

You saw Fat Fox disguised as Granny."

"Prove it," said Fat Fox.

"Very simple," said Gumshoe.

He took Clue Number Three

out of his pocket.

"I found these glasses in the

henhouse," he said.

"They're Granny Fox's.

And Granny can't see without them.

So she wouldn't have left them

at the scene of the crime.

You made one mistake, Fat Fox.

You dropped Granny's glasses

when you made your getaway."

"Curses!" growled Fat Fox.

"Good work, Gumshoe!"
said Inspector Goose.
"I have caught the kidnapper!
The next time I need help,
I will call on you."

The Inspector locked up Fat Fox.

"What's for dinner?" asked Fat Fox.

"Bread and water,"

said Inspector Goose.

"Double curses!" growled Fat Fox.

Gumshoe Goose went to his office.

He opened his black book to

the Case of the Hungry Kidnapper.

Then he wrote: CASE CLOSED.

"Catching kidnappers is hard

work," he said.

"I think I will rest my eyes."

Zzzzzzzz, snored Gumshoe Goose.

DATE DUE

DEMCO, INC. 38-3011

For Kendra
M.K.

Published by Dial Books for Young Readers
A Division of NAL Penguin Inc.
2 Park Avenue
New York, New York 10016

Published simultaneously in Canada by
Fitzhenry & Whiteside Limited, Toronto

Text copyright © 1988 by Mary DeBall Kwitz
Pictures copyright © 1988 by Lisa Campbell Ernst
All rights reserved
Printed in Hong Kong by South China Printing Co.
The Dial Easy-to-Read logo is a registered trademark of
Dial Books for Young Readers, a division of NAL Penguin Inc.
® TM 1,162,718.

Library of Congress Cataloging in Publication Data
Kwitz, Mary DeBall. Gumshoe Goose, private eye.
Summary: Detective Gumshoe Goose helps his father,
Inspector Goose, solve the case of the hungry kidnapper.
[1. Mystery and detective stories. 2. Geese—Fiction.]
I. Ernst, Lisa Campbell, ill. II. Title.
PZ7.K976Gu 1988   [E]   86-29331
ISBN 0-8037-0423-2
ISBN 0-8037-0424-0 (lib. bdg.)

First Edition
(a)
1 3 5 7 9 10 8 6 4 2

The full-color artwork was produced using pen and ink
and pastels. It was then color-separated and reproduced
as red, blue, yellow, and black halftones.

Reading Level 2.1

JF Kwitz
Kwitz, Mary DeBall.
Gumshoe Goose, private eye

SEP 1999
RECEIVED
OHIO DOMINICAN
COLLEGE LIBRARY
COLUMBUS, OHIO
43219

by Mary DeBall Kwitz
pictures by Lisa Campbell Ernst

DIAL BOOKS FOR YOUNG READERS
NEW YORK